If I Was a Banana

Written by Alexandra Tylee

Illustrated by Kieran Rynhart

GECKO PRESS

If I was a banana I would be that one,
all yellow and fat and full of banana.

If I was a mountain I would be the one
with the snow and the clouds
and the rumbling volcano
that never blows its top
(well, never enough to hurt anyone).

If I had to be a bird I would be big,
with huge wings and a long neck.

You would only ever see me
in the distance, flying away somewhere
on my own, looking very regal.

If I was a cow
I would
want to be
the one
standing
over there.

That cow makes you feel like there is nothing more
important than being a black cow standing on green grass.

If I was a cloud it would be great to be
a big black storm cloud and shoot lightning,
thunder, and hail all over the place.

But then, maybe a much smaller,

lighter, fluffy sort of cloud

would be a better sort of cloud to be.

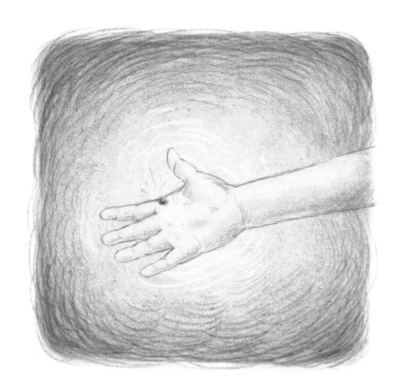

If I was a ladybug
I don't know how
I would feel.
To be that small
could be a little
frightening.

And then, who knows,
maybe I would be
a very brave,
bright red ladybug,
and fly very high
without a care in the world.

If I was a fish
I would not like it very much.
I don't want to be a fish.

Maybe being a whale would be all right for
a while, but I would rather not be a fish.

If I was an elephant
I think I would
have to be very
careful where
I put my feet.

I guess you would
get used to that.

It would be good to be an elephant,
to be big and strong and free in Africa.

If I was a spoon
I would be that one–
perfectly shaped and worn,
with the silver fading
in all the right places.

I know it seems odd,
the thought of being a spoon,
but I think I might quite like it.

If I was a star I would be that one,
the little one,
just above that other star.
It is smiling at me
and is quite different from all the others.

If I was a tree
I would be quite happy.
No matter how old I got,
of all the things I could be,
a tree seems to be one of the best.

If I was a cat I would be white all over
and aloof and hardly ever purr,
except for you, and then I would make
such a noise that they would come and see
what all the commotion was about.

If I was a lion I would be that one over there,
deep in thought, sitting with its friend.

If I was a lion you might
not want to talk to me,
so I won't be a lion.

If I was a little boy,

or a big one, which I am

–well, not really big but not really little either–

I think of all the boys I could be,
I am most comfortable being

me.

This edition first published in 2016 by Gecko Press
PO Box 9335, Marion Square, Wellington 6141, New Zealand
info@geckopress.com

Text © Alexandra Tylee 2016
Illustrations © Kieran Rynhart 2016

Distributed in the United States and Canada by Lerner Publishing Group, www.lernerbooks.com
Distributed in the UK by Bounce Sales & Marketing, www.bouncemarketing.co.uk
Distributed in Australia by Scholastic Australia, www.scholastic.com.au
Distributed in New Zealand by Upstart Distribution, www.upstartpress.co.nz

Designed by Vida & Luke Kelly, New Zealand
Printed in China by Everbest Printing Co Ltd,
an accredited ISO 14001 & FSC certified printer

ISBN hardback: 978-1-776570-33-1
ISBN paperback: 978-1-776570-34-8
Ebook available

For more curiously good books, visit www.geckopress.com